Incredible

ME!

By Kathi Appelt   Pictures by G. Brian Karas

HARPERCOLLINS PUBLISHERS

Incredible Me!
Text copyright © 2003 by Kathi Appelt
Illustrations copyright © 2003 by G. Brian Karas
Manufactured in China. All rights reserved.
www.harperchildrens.com

Library of Congress Cataloging-in-Publication Data
Appelt, Kathi.
    Incredible me! / by Kathi Appelt ; pictures by G. Brian Karas.
        p.   cm.
    Summary: A girl celebrates her own individuality, from her freckles to her wiggles.
    ISBN 0-06-028622-9 — ISBN 0-06-028623-7 (lib. bdg.)
    [1. Individuality—Fiction. 2. Self-esteem—Fiction. 3. Stories in rhyme.] I. Karas, G.
Brian, ill. II. Title.
PZ8.3.A554 In 2003   2001039681
[E]—dc21   CIP
                                                                          AC

Typography by Matt Adamec
1 2 3 4 5 6 7 8 9 10
❖
First Edition

To Alexander and Simone—the kit and caboodle!
With love, K.A.

For Jamie
—G.B.K.

Nobody has my singular nose

Nobody tips on **my** ten toes

Nobody wears a smile like this

Nobody blows the kiss I kiss

I'm the cat's meow,

I'm the dog's top flea

I'm the **one**, the **only**,

most marvelous **Me!**

Nobody cries with my big tears

Nobody hears with my two ears

Nobody giggles like little ol' me

Nobody sees the way I see

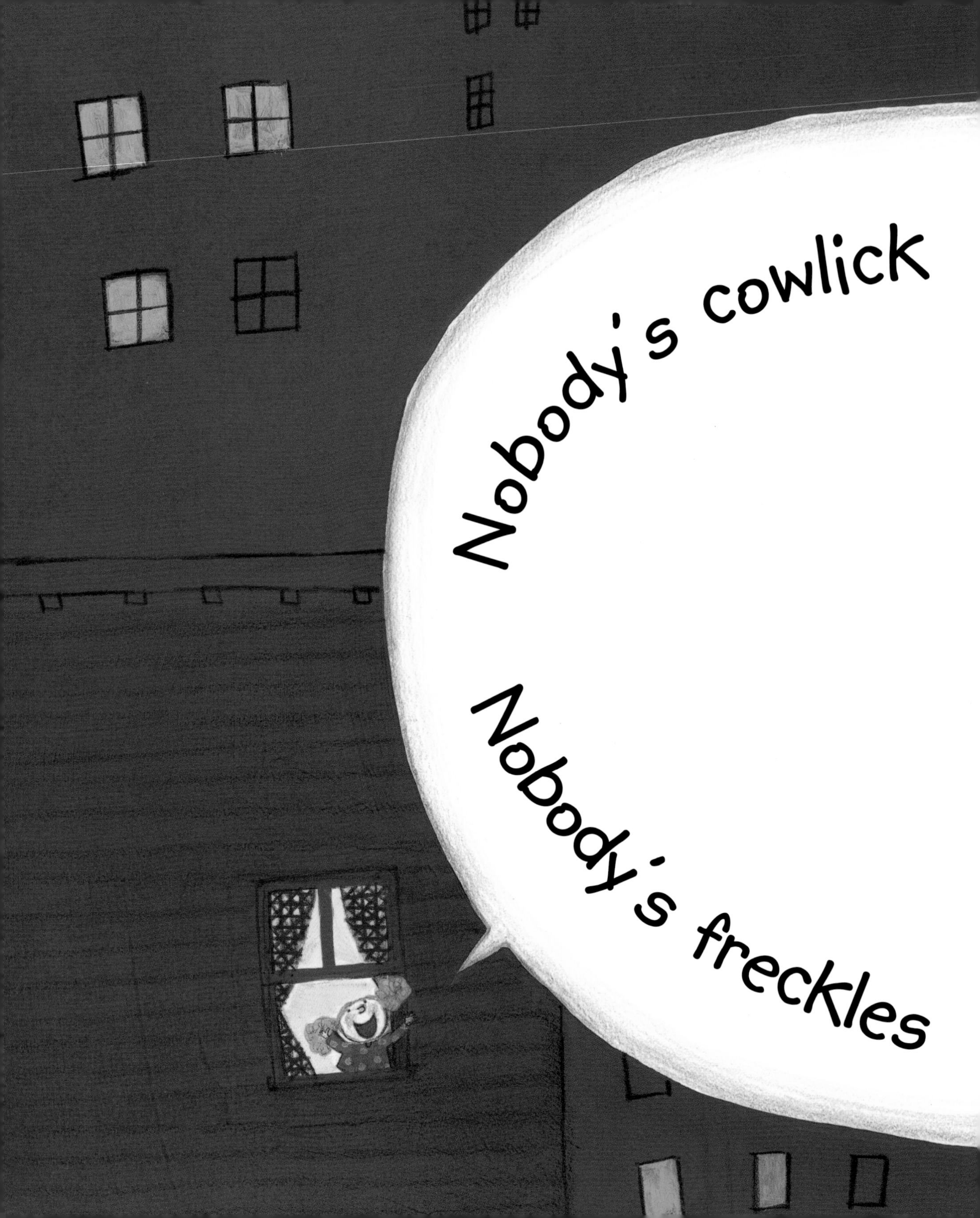
Nobody's cowlick
Nobody's freckles

stands up like mine

are this divine

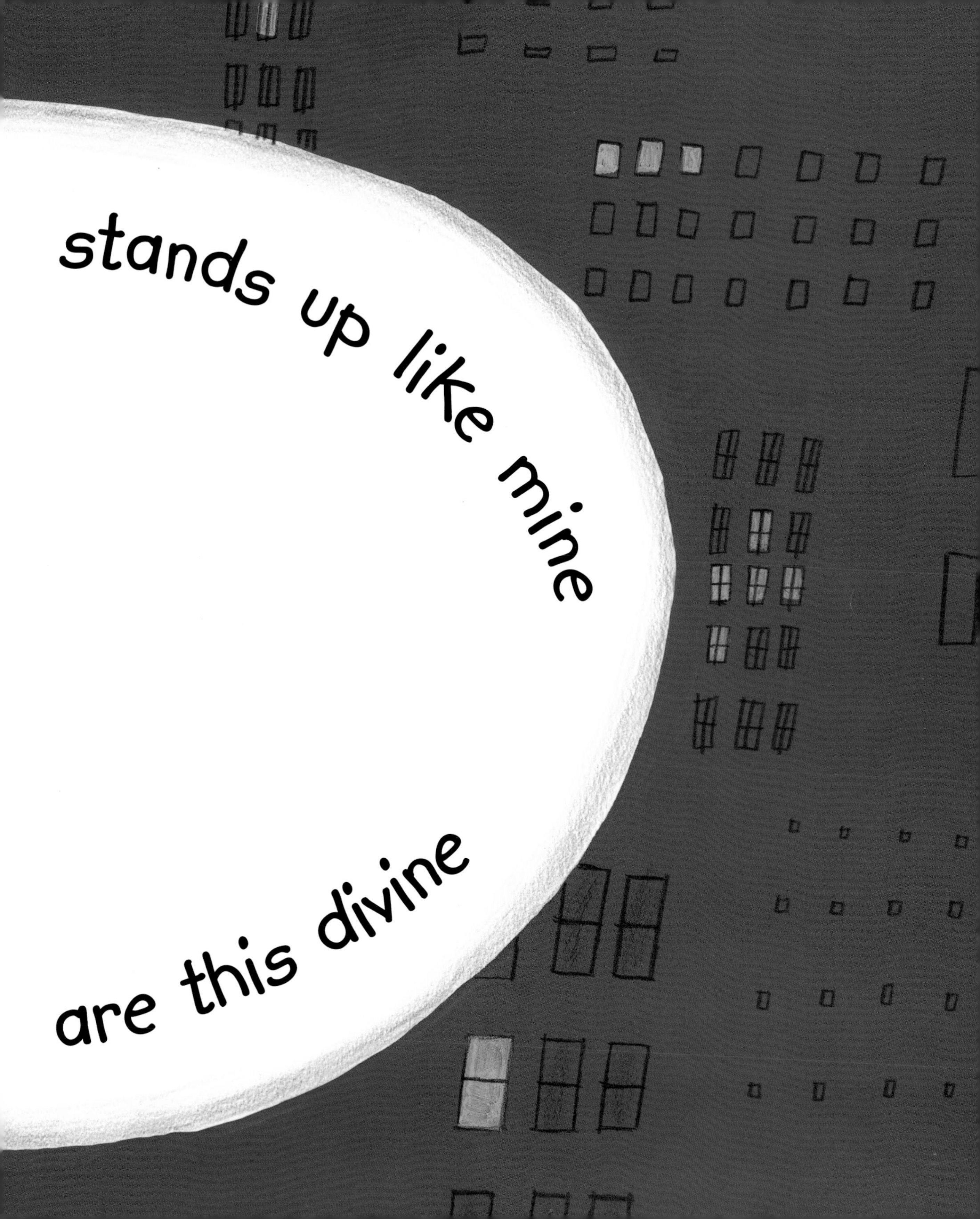

I'm the cream in the butter,
I'm the salt in the sea
I'm the one, the only, spectacular Me!

Nobody sings the way I sing

Nobody shares the dreams I dream

Nobody waltzes on my two feet

Nobody sits on my round seat

Nobody, **nobody** knows what I know

Nobody goes every place that I go

I'm the dill in the pickle,
the sweet in the pea
I'm the one, the only, adorable Me!

Nobody marches in my two boots

Nobody itches in my new suit

It's a fact, it's certain,
I'm the kit and caboodle

I'm the beat in the jazz,

I'm the jam in the strudel

I'm the pearl in the oyster, the A to the Z

I'm the one, the only, incredible